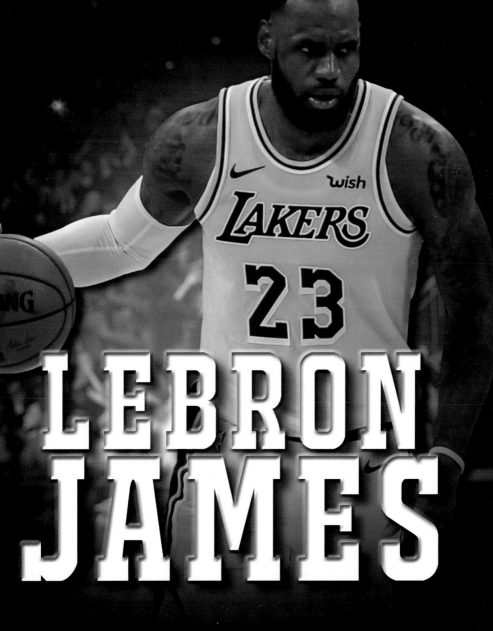

HARDWOOD GREATS

PRO BASKETBALL'S BEST PLAYERS

LEBRON JAMES

HARDWOOD GREATS

PRO BASKETBALL'S BEST PLAYERS

CHRIS PAUL

GIANNIS ANTETOKOUNMPO

JAMES HARDEN

KEVIN DURANT

LEBRON JAMES

PAUL GEORGE

RUSSELL WESTBROOK

STEPHEN CURRY

HARDWOOD GREATS
PRO BASKETBALL'S BEST PLAYERS

LEBRON JAMES

DONALD PARKER

MASON CREST
PHILADELPHIA
MIAMI

Mason Crest
450 Parkway Drive, Suite D
Broomall, Pennsylvania 19008
(866) MCP-BOOK (toll-free)
www.masoncrest.com

First printing
9 8 7 6 5 4 3 2 1

ISBN (hardback) 978-1-4222-4349-7
ISBN (series) 978-1-4222-4344-2
ISBN (ebook) 978-1-4222-7464-4

Cataloging-in-Publication Data on file with the Library of Congress

Developed and Produced by National Highlights Inc.
Editor: Andrew Luke
Interior and cover design: Annalisa Gumbrecht, Studio Gumbrecht
Production: Michelle Luke

QR CODES AND LINKS TO THIRD-PARTY CONTENT

CONTENTS

KEY ICONS TO LOOK FOR:

 Words To Understand: These words with their easy-to-understand definitions will increase the reader's understanding of the text while building vocabulary skills.

 Sidebars: This boxed material within the main text allows readers to build knowledge, gain insights, explore possibilities, and broaden their perspectives by weaving together additional information to provide realistic and holistic perspectives.

 Educational Videos: Readers can view videos by scanning our QR codes, providing them with additional educational content to supplement the text. Examples include news coverage, moments in history, speeches, iconic sports moments, and much more!

 Text-Dependent Questions: These questions send the reader back to the text for more careful attention to the evidence presented there.

 Research Projects: Readers are pointed toward areas of further inquiry connected to each chapter. Suggestions are provided for projects that encourage deeper research and analysis.

 Series Glossary of Key Terms: This back-of-the-book glossary contains terminology used throughout this series. Words found here increase the reader's ability to read and comprehend higher level books and articles in this field.

WORDS TO UNDERSTAND

Midas: A legendary Phrygian king who is given the power of turning everything he touches to gold

plateau: To reach a level, period, or condition of stability or maximum attainment

prodigy: A highly talented child or youth

stint: A period of time spent at a particular activity

surpassed: Became better, greater, or stronger than

CHAPTER 1

GREATEST MOMENTS

THE CAREER OF LEBRON JAMES

What can be said about LeBron James that has not already been said? He has become, in 16 NBA (National Basketball Association) seasons through 2018–2019, "King James," arguably the greatest individual to have ever played in the NBA. He was a highly touted prodigy in the sport, destined to play basketball at Ohio State University after coming out of Akron, Ohio's St. Vincent–St. Mary High School. Instead, James chose to be drafted by the Cleveland Cavaliers in the 2003 NBA draft. He was taken in the draft as the first overall pick.

Since joining the NBA, James has risen through the ranks to become regarded as one of the best of the best. In 16 seasons he has scored more than 30,000 points, and is the youngest in NBA history to reach the 10,000–, 20,000–, and 30,000–point scoring marks. James, in fact, is only one of eight players that has played in the NBA who has scored at least 30,000 career points.

James led the Cavaliers to five Eastern Conference championships in 11 seasons.

For his career to date, James has become the first player to also post more than 8,000 rebounds and assists, having grabbed 8,415 boards and dished 8,208 assists. He has established himself as a premier scoring threat, both inside and outside the three-point line. The 2017–2018 NBA season saw James lead the league in minutes played and minutes per game, field goals (857), and points scored (2,251). He helped lead his Cleveland Cavaliers to a fifth Eastern Conference championship and the NBA Finals, where they came up short to the Golden State Warriors.

Known around the league as King James, he has had the Midas touch when it comes to winning and bringing out the very best in his teammates. James has played alongside great players like Chris Bosh, Dwyane Wade, and Kyrie Irving. His style of play encourages other players to step up their games and play to win, an attitude that has helped bring championships to Cleveland and Miami.

Along with his scoring ability, James has brought a level of professionalism to the game that has not been seen for some time. He has not only excelled on the court through his play, but he has also transferred his skills on the court to his activities off the court. James has appeared in movies and on television and has created a marketing brand promoting shoes, soft drinks, clothing, and other products.

There is no question that as soon as James is done playing professional basketball and his name comes up for consideration for the Hall of Fame, LeBron James will receive 100 percent of the votes. His name is mentioned alongside legends like Michael Jordan, Wilt Chamberlain, Kareem Abdul-Jabbar, and Larry Bird as one of the game's all-time greats!

JAMES' GREATEST CAREER MOMENTS

HERE IS A LIST OF

SOME OF THE CAREER

FIRSTS AND GREATEST

ACHIEVEMENTS DURING

HIS TIME IN THE NBA:

James is certain to be a unanimous choice to enter the Basketball Hall of Fame when he retires.

FIRST NBA CHAMPIONSHIP (2012)

James spent the first seven seasons of his NBA career with the Cleveland Cavaliers. During his time in Cleveland, he led the Cavs to their appearance in the NBA Finals in 2007. After losing to the San Antonio Spurs four games to none, James developed a hunger to return to the championship game and claim his place alongside the league's champions. He got his chance for redemption in his second season playing for the Miami Heat in 2012. James led the way in a showdown against the Oklahoma City Thunder, averaging 28.6 points a game, to win the first of his three championship trophies.

Highlights of the 2012 NBA regular season and Finals MVP (most valuable player) LeBron James leading the Miami Heat to their franchise second and his first NBA championship.

POINTS IN A CAREER: 20,000

James holds the NBA record as the youngest player to score 10,000 points in a career, which he set in 2007. Six years later he set the career record as the youngest player to score 20,000 points, in a January 16, 2013, game against the Golden State Warriors at just over twenty-eight years of age. The name of the player he **surpassed**? Kobe Bryant of the Los Angeles Lakers, who set the previous record at twenty-nine years, four months old.

James, as a member of the Miami Heat in a January 16, 2013, game versus Golden State scored a total of 25 points, along with 10 assists and seven rebounds. His performance makes him one of 48 players (as of the end of the 2017–2018 season) in NBA history to score at least 20,000 points in his career.

only the eighth player to reach this **plateau**. He is also the only player in NBA history with more than 30,000 points, 8,000 assists, and 8,000 rebounds in a career.

James turns in a 28-point game against the Spurs on January 23, 2018, to become the eighth player in NBA history to reach 30,000 points. As of the end of the 2018–2019 season, James had scored 32,543 points, which ranked him fourth all-time and within 5,844 points of the all-time leader, Kareem Abdul-Jabbar, a former Milwaukee Buck and Los Angeles Laker.

FIRST PLAYER TO AVERAGE A TRIPLE-DOUBLE IN AN NBA FINAL (NBA RECORD)

The 2017 NBA Finals saw LeBron James' triumphant return to the championship game, after leading the Cavaliers to the NBA championship in the 2016 finals (against the same opponent, the Golden State Warriors). Although he was unable to lead his Cavaliers to a repeat championship, his 33.6-point average, 12 total rebounds, and 10 assists made him the first player in the history of the NBA to average a triple-double.

Here's an analysis of LeBron James' performance in the 2017 NBA Finals against the Golden State Warriors where he became the first NBA player to average a triple-double in the championship series.

61 POINTS IN A GAME

In a March 3, 2014, game against the Charlotte Bobcats (while a member of the Miami Heat), James scored 61 points. The game resulted in a 124–107 victory as James made his first eight three-point shots for 24 points, as well as nine free throws (9 points) and 14 two-pointers (28 points). His 61 points make him one of only 25 players in the history of the NBA to score at least 60 points in a game.

Watch a shot-by-shot video of LeBron James scoring 61 points against the Charlotte Bobcats in a March 3, 2014, game. The performance ranks tied for the 43rd most points scored by an NBA player in a game in the history of the Association.

FIRST NBA CHAMPIONSHIP AS A MEMBER OF THE CLEVELAND CAVALIERS (2016)

James returned to Cleveland for the start of the 2014–2015 NBA season after spending four seasons playing in Miami where he won back-to-back championships (2012, 2013). He came back on a mission to bring a championship trophy of any kind to Cleveland, the first since the 1964 Cleveland Browns NFL championship win. A depleted Cavaliers squad lost the 2015 championship in six games to the Golden State Warriors. They regrouped and in 2016, facing the same Warriors team and down three games to one, came back to win the series and the championship in seven games.

Check out a clip featuring the last three-plus minutes of LeBron James leading the Cavaliers to a dramatic Game 7 victory in the 2016 NBA Finals over the Golden State Warriors, June 19, 2016.

FIRST MVP AWARD: 2008-2009 NBA SEASON

James, in his sixth season in the league, at the age of twenty-four, won the NBA's Most Valuable Player. He accomplished this while averaging 28.4 points per game, 7.6 total rebounds, and 7.25 assists. He led or was near the top in nearly every offensive category, including two- and three-pointers made, free throws made, assists, and rebounds. He finished the season in MVP style with a playoff run where he averaged 7.29 assists, 9.14 rebounds, and 35.29 points per game.

Video highlights of James' 2008–2009 NBA season, which ended with his winning the 2009 NBA Most Valuable Player award, the

THREE-TIME NBA FINALS MVP (2012, 2013, 2016)

James has appeared in the NBA Finals nine times, in 2007, and then eight straight years from 2011 to 2018, winning three times and losing six. He has been named Finals MVP, an award first given out in 1969 to Los Angeles Lakers guard Jerry West, three times, an accomplishment that has been made only by James and four other players (Tim Duncan, Magic Johnson, Shaquille O'Neal, and Michael Jordan, who leads the way with six).

Video of LeBron James after winning the NBA championship with his Miami Heat teammates in 2012, receiving the 2012 NBA Final MVP Trophy from Bill Russell.

James traditionally wears number 23, but switched to number 6 with Miami because the Heat have retired #23 in tribute to Michael Jordan.

JAMES

6

TEXT-DEPENDENT QUESTIONS

1. Which NBA player did James surpass to become the youngest to score 20,000 points in a career?

2. How many league Most Valuable Player awards has he won in his 16 years playing in the NBA?

3. How many total points has he scored as an NBA player through the end of the 2017–2018 season?

RESEARCH PROJECT

Scoring 30,000 points in a career is something that only seven other players have accomplished in the NBA. James is the only active player to score 30,000 points in his career. He is the youngest to reach this milestone, having passed Kobe Bryant of the Los Angeles Lakers. Looking at the seven players who have reached 30,000 points, rank them in order of age first when they reached that mark and then by number of seasons played before scoring that many points.

WORDS TO UNDERSTAND

amass: To collect for oneself

hone: To make more acute, intense, or effective

synonymous: Having the same connotations, implications, or reference

transcend: To rise above or go beyond the limits of

CHAPTER 2

THE ROAD TO THE TOP

LEBRON JAMES ON THE COURT

LeBron James' name has become synonymous with greatness in 16 seasons. King James has transcended many of the best players in the history of the game to take his place on top of the NBA throne. His numbers are on par with those of some of the greatest individuals to ever play the game, including Michael Jordan, Wilt Chamberlain, and Kobe Bryant. James is at or near the top of almost every scoring category and, at age thirty-four, has more to add to his growing list of accomplishments.

When you think about the NBA, you think about his play on the court. You think about the way James leads his team and gets everyone involved or the way he puts a game on his back in order to dictate the outcome. His efforts have resulted in 14 all-star appearances in 16 seasons. He has been named the MVP of three all-star games (2006, 2008, 2018) and three NBA Finals (2012, 2013, 2016).

James is the youngest player ever to score at least 30,000 career points in the NBA.

James is on pace to exceed the performance of many of the great players in the history of the NBA. There is no telling how much greater he can become, but a look at his numbers shows that he has come very far, and fairly quickly. Here is how he stacks up against some of the all-time greats in the league's history:

PLAYER	PTS	PPG	FG	FG%	3PT	3PT%	FT	FT%
Kareem Abdul-Jabbar*	38,387	24.6	15,837	0.000	1	0.056	6,712	0.721
Karl Malone*	36,928	25.0	13,528	0.516	85	0.274	9,787	0.742
Kobe Bryant	33,643	25.0	11,719	0.447	1827	0.329	8,378	0.837
Michael Jordan*	32,292	30.1	12,192	0.497	581	0.327	7,327	0.835
Wilt Chamberlain*	31,419	30.1	12,681	0.540	0	0.000	6,057	0.511
LeBron James	*32,543*	*27.2*	*11,838*	*0.504*	*1,727*	*0.343*	*7,140*	*0.736*
Julius Erving*	30,026	24.2	11,818	0.506	134	0.298	6,256	0.777
Oscar Robertson*	26,710	25.7	9,508	0.485	0	0.000	7,694	0.838
Jerry West*	25,192	27.0	9,016	0.474	0	0.000	7,160	0.814
Larry Bird*	21,791	24.3	8,591	0.496	649	0.376	3,960	0.886

* Members of Basketball Hall of Fame.

James was voted MVP of the annual McDonald's All-American Game for high school standouts in 2003.

NBA DRAFT DAY 2009 SIGNIFICANT ACCOUNTS

- LeBron James was selected by Cleveland with the first pick in the first round of the 2003 NBA draft.

- The 2003 NBA draft was held at Madison Square Garden located in New York City on June 26, 2003.

- The 2003 NBA draft featured four members of the 2008 U.S. Olympic Gold-Medal Team that played in Beijing, China: LeBron James, Carmelo Anthony, Chris Bosh, and Dwyane Wade. They were the first four Americans picked in the draft, all in the top five.

- The 2003 draft also featured James' future Los Angeles Lakers coach, Luke Walton, who was selected by the Lakers with the 32nd pick.

- James was one of three high school players picked in the 2003 draft. Ndudi Ebi from Westbury Christian High School in Houston went 26th to Minnesota, and James Lang of Central Park Christian High School in Birmingham, Alabama, went 49th to Indiana.

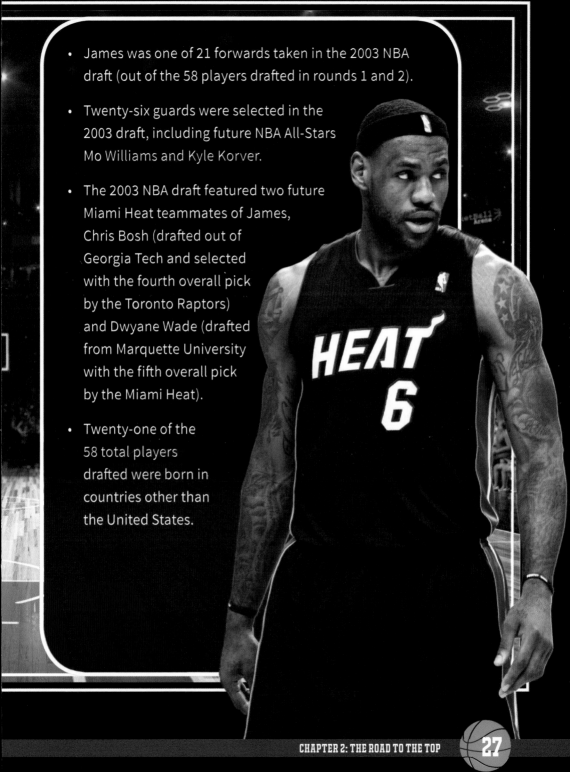

- James was one of 21 forwards taken in the 2003 NBA draft (out of the 58 players drafted in rounds 1 and 2).

- Twenty-six guards were selected in the 2003 draft, including future NBA All-Stars Mo Williams and Kyle Korver.

- The 2003 NBA draft featured two future Miami Heat teammates of James, Chris Bosh (drafted out of Georgia Tech and selected with the fourth overall pick by the Toronto Raptors) and Dwyane Wade (drafted from Marquette University with the fifth overall pick by the Miami Heat).

- Twenty-one of the 58 total players drafted were born in countries other than the United States.

James excelled at the high school level, quickly gaining national exposure. He was named Ohio Mr. Basketball three times, in his sophomore, junior, and senior years while attending St. Vincent–St. Mary High School (Fighting Irish) in his hometown of Akron, Ohio. He was also named the 2003 McDonald's All-American Game MVP in his senior year. James was such a phenomenon that some of his high school games were nationally televised or available through pay-per-view, and many were played at a nearby university arena to accommodate the huge demand for tickets.

James is ranked in the Ohio High School Athletic Association record books (unofficially) as the fifth all-time career scorer and is tied at 22nd in the state for highest field-goal percentage for a career (based on a minimum of 55 percent and 800 field-goal attempts) at 55.9 percent.

High school is where James honed his skills, the skills he has expanded since joining the NBA in 2003. He played four years of varsity basketball for the Fighting Irish, accumulating the following statistics:

(season totals including playoffs)

Year (G)	PTS	PPG	FGM/A	FG%	3PTM/A	3PT%	FTM/A	FT%
1999–2000 (27)	487	18.0	199-386	51.6	30-95	31.6	59-74	79.7
2000–2001 (27)	684	25.3	264-352	58.4	33-84	39.3	123-173	71.1
2001–2002 (27)	756	28.0	300-531	56.5	48-141	34.0	108-182	59.3
2002–2003 (24)	730	30.4	295-527	56.0	60-157	38.2	80-118	67.8
TOTALS	**1309**	**19.0**	**417**	**824**	**102**	**271**	**373**	**494**

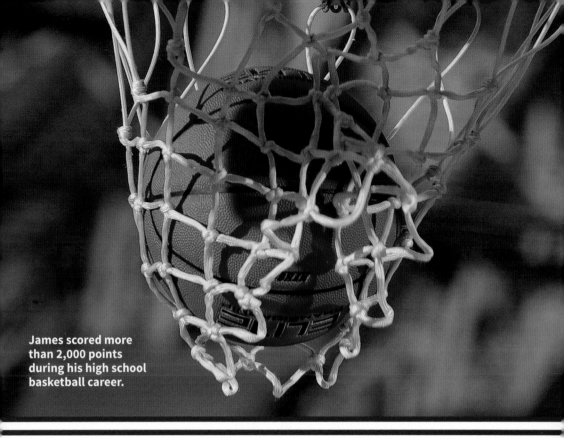

James scored more than 2,000 points during his high school basketball career.

James *amassed* several honors over his four-year high school career:

- All-Ohio Division III First Team (2000, 2001)

- All-Ohio Division II First Team (2002, 2003)

- *Cleveland Plain Dealer* Best of the Best (2000)

- *Cleveland Plain Dealer* Player of the Year (2001, 2002, 2003)

- Ohio State Tournament MVP (2000, 2001, 2003)

- *USA Today* First Team (2001–2003)

- *USA Today* Player of the Year (2002)

- Gatorade National Basketball Player of the Year (2002, 2003)

- Gatorade National Athlete of the Year (2003)

- Ohio Mr. Basketball (2001, 2002, 2003)

HIGH SCHOOL GREAT
TO HARDWOOD SUPERSTAR

James entered St. Vincent–St. Mary High School—nicknamed the Fighting Irish—in his hometown of Akron, Ohio, in 1999. He played not only basketball but also football—as a wide receiver—and was even recruited by Notre Dame University, the other Fighting Irish, as he was thought to be a potential future NFL prospect. Focusing on basketball, he was named Ohio Mr. Basketball three times as a sophomore, junior, and senior, was a two-time national player of the year as a junior and senior, and led his undefeated Irish to a Division III state title in his freshman year. James went from averaging 18 points per game (ppg) as a freshman, to 30 ppg as a senior. His teams won 101 games and lost only six times, an incredible winning percentage of 94.3 percent. It is no wonder James made the immediate jump to the NBA from high school!

A highlight video of some of James' greatest moments as a member of the St. Vincent–St. Mary's "Fighting Irish" basketball team. His play on the court was the beginning of his legend as one of the greatest to ever play the game of basketball.

COLLEGE

After his senior year at St. Vincent–St. Mary High School, James decided to declare for the 2003 NBA draft. At the time of this decision, James was a highly sought after collegiate prospect. He received seven offers to play NCAA Division I-level basketball at the following schools:

- Duke University (nicknamed "Blue Devils")

- Louisville University (nicknamed "Cardinals")

- Michigan State University (nicknamed "Spartans")

- The Ohio State University (nicknamed "Buckeyes")

- University of Florida (nicknamed "Gators")

- University of Kentucky (nicknamed "Wildcats")

- University of North Carolina (nicknamed "Tar Heels")

James ultimately decided to forego college and instead declared himself eligible for the 2003 NBA draft.

James might have played at Duke University's Cameron Indoor Stadium had he decided to accept one of the several offers he received for a college scholarship.

NBA DRAFT DAY 2003

James declared for the 2003 NBA draft after completing his senior year in high school. He did not participate in the 2003 NBA Pre-Draft Combine. His pre-draft measurements were:

six feet eight inches (2.03 m), 222 pounds (111.13 kg)

LEBRON JAMES VS. OTHER TOP DRAFT PICKS

James was one of 58 players taken in the 2003 NBA draft. He was selected number one overall by the Cleveland Cavaliers, considered his hometown team. Through 16 seasons through 2019 James leads (or is near the top of) his draft class in many statistical categories, including:

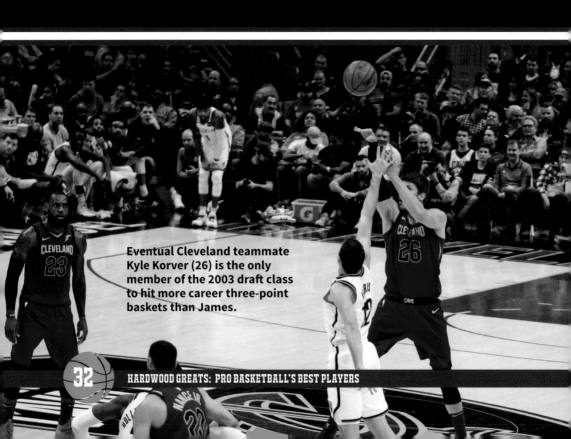

Eventual Cleveland teammate Kyle Korver (26) is the only member of the 2003 draft class to hit more career three-point baskets than James.

THREE-POINT FG MADE		ASSISTS	
Kyle Korver	2,351	**LeBron James**	**8,662**
LeBron James	**1,727**	Dwyane Wade	5,701
Carmelo Anthony	1,362	Kirk Hinrich	4,245
Kirk Hinrich	1,172	Mo Williams	3,990
Mo Williams	1,094	Luke Ridnour	3,713

FIELD GOALS MADE		REBOUNDS	
LeBron James	**11,838**	**LeBron James**	**8,880**
Carmelo Anthony	9,137	Chris Bosh	7,592
Dwyane Wade	8,454	Carmelo Anthony	6,938
Chris Bosh	6,209	David West	6,590
David West	5,703	ZaZa Pachulia	6,315

James has more than 8,000 career total each of both rebounds and assists.

Former Laker Luke Walton was drafted along with James in 2003 and ended up coaching James in his first season in Los Angeles.

LEBRON JAMES AND THE MIAMI "BIG THREE"

When James joined the Miami Heat for the 2010–2011 season, it was the beginning of a mini-dynasty for the team. The dynasty came into being through the free agency of James and fellow 2003 draft pick, Chris Bosh. Bosh, who was originally drafted fourth overall by the Toronto Raptors, joined James and Miami Heat star Dwyane Wade (drafted fifth overall in 2003) to form the "Big Three." As Heat teammates, the trio appeared in four NBA Finals (2011–2014), winning in 2012 and 2013. Here's how these players stack up to each other in their careers:

PLAYER	PTS	PPG	FGM	FG%	3PTM	3PT%	FTM	FT%
LeBron James	32,543	27.2	11,838	50.4	1,727	34.3	7,140	73.6
Dwyane Wade	23,165	22	8,454	48.0	549	29.3	5,708	76.5
Chris Bosh	17,189	19.2	6,209	49.4	305	33.5	4,466	79.9

JAMES AND LAKERS COACH LUKE WALTON

While James was the number-one overall pick in the 2003 draft, the son of another number-one overall pick was taken with the third pick in the second round (32nd overall). Luke Walton, whose father Bill Walton was the number-one pick in the 1974 NBA draft, played 10 seasons in the league, from 2003–2012 with the Los Angeles Lakers and then with the Cleveland Cavaliers (2012–2013), after James left Cleveland for the Miami Heat.

After his career ended, Walton went on to become an assistant coach with the Memphis Grizzlies and Golden State Warriors. While a coach with the Warriors, his team defeated the James-led Cavaliers to win the 2015 NBA championship. Walton was named coach of the Los Angeles Lakers in April of 2016. James announced in July of 2018 that he was joining the Lakers as a free agent, where his coach was a member of his own draft class and someone James played against in the league. Walton resigned as Lakers coach in 2019 and took the head coaching job in Sacramento.

His accomplishments in high school and the pros have placed James in the ranks of the greatest players in the history of the game of basketball. His presence in the NBA has elevated the league to a new level. There have been few players that have come into the league before James with his level of talent, and it may be another generation or two before you see a talent quite like his again in the NBA.

Darius Songaila tries to guard James in a 2008 game against the Wizards.

TEXT-DEPENDENT QUESTIONS

1. What two players drafted in 2003 with LeBron James became teammates of his in 2010 with the Miami Heat?

2. What Los Angeles Lakers head coach was drafted in 2003 along with James?

3. What are the names of three of the seven schools that recruited James to play basketball at the collegiate level?

 # RESEARCH PROJECT

James made the jump from high school basketball to the NBA. Name five other players who within the past 10 years (2008–2018) have played in the NBA (at least 100 games) after being drafted from high school.

WORDS TO UNDERSTAND

approximate: Nearly correct or exact: close in value or amount but not precise

astonish: To cause a feeling of great wonder or surprise in (someone)

embodies: To represent (something) in a clear and obvious way; to be a symbol or example of (something)

reclaim: To regain possession of

CHAPTER 3

ON THE COURT

NBA ACCOMPLISHMENTS

LeBron James, or King James as he is often called, has established himself as one of the NBA's greatest of all time (G.O.A.T.). This is clear with even a quick look at some of his important statistics during his time in the NBA, beginning with scoring. James is fourth all-time in the NBA in career points scored. James is the youngest player in league to score 30,000 or more points in a career. Based on his season average of 2,069 points, it will take James approximately 291 games (three and a half seasons) to reach former Milwaukee Buck and Los Angeles Laker Kareem Abdul-Jabbar's all-time record of 38,387 points.

LEBRON JAMES

GUARD/FORWARD

- Date of birth: December 30, 1984

- Height: six feet eight inches (2.03 m) Weight: Approx. 250 pounds (113 kg)

- Drafted in the first round of the 2003 NBA draft (first pick overall) by the Cleveland Cavaliers

- Three-time NBA champion (2012, 2013, 2016)

- Four-time NBA MVP (2009, 2010, 2012, 2013)

- Three-time NBA Finals MVP (2012, 2013, 2016)

- Fifteen-time NBA All-Star

- 2004 NBA Rookie of the Year

- 2008 NBA scoring champion

- Twelve-time All-NBA first team

If he maintains his current scoring pace, James will become the NBA career points leader in 2023.

James has recorded 81 triple-doubles in his career.

KING JAMES

James has averaged 27.2 points per game over his 16-year career and played in 1,198 games (as of the end of the 2018–2019). This number ranks James fourth all-time in career ppg, well behind Michael Jordan's 30.12 ppg, but first on the active player list, just ahead of Golden State Warrior's small forward Kevin Durant, who has an average of 27.02. James has posted 238 point-assist double-doubles in his career. This ranks him 15th in the NBA. He also has an astonishing 81 triple-doubles, which is any combination of points, assists, rebounds, and steals. His 81 triple-doubles are fifth best in NBA history.

James, in addition to his career triple-doubles mark, has recorded 13 in a single season. This accomplishment ties him for 13th on the NBA all-time list for a single season. He also holds the NBA career mark for the most triple-doubles in an NBA Finals with 10; the next best total is eight, recorded by Magic Johnson. LeBron James has a career that has been rivaled by only a few players in the history of the NBA. When you mention his name, it is not hard to place him in such company as G.O.A.T. candidates like Wilt Chamberlain, Michael Jordan, Larry Bird, and Kareem Abdul-Jabbar, among all NBA players.

James has played for his country in three Olympic Summer Games and won two gold medals.

LEBRON JAMES' HONORS AND AWARDS

James has earned many honors and awards in his 16-year NBA career (through the end of the 2018–2019 season). Here is a list of some of those accomplishments:

- James is a three-time *Sporting News* MVP (2006, 2009, 2010) and was named the *Sporting News* Rookie of the Year (2004).

- He was named to the NBA All-Defensive first team five times (2009–2013) and to the NBA All-Defensive second team in 2014.

- James received the J. Walter Kennedy Citizenship Award in 2017.

- He is a two-time AP Athlete of the Year (2013, 2016).

- James was twice named *Sports Illustrated* Sportsperson of the Year (2012, 2016).

- He was named the USA Basketball Male Athlete of the Year (2012).

- James was a member of three US Men's Basketball Olympic teams: Athens (2004–Bronze), Beijing (2008–Gold), London (2012–Gold).

SECOND ATHLETE TO RECEIVE SPORTS ILLUSTRATED SPORTSPERSON OF THE YEAR TWO TIMES

James accomplished a feat that only golfer Tiger Woods has done before—in 2016 he became a two-time recipient of the *Sports Illustrated* (*SI*) annual award, Sportsperson of the Year. He had previously been honored with the award in 2012. The award, given out by *SI* since 1954, recognizes "the athlete or team whose performance that year most **embodies** the spirit of sportsmanship and achievement." Interestingly, these two sports legends (James and Woods) share the same birthday, December 30.

LeBron James was named 2016 Sportsperson of the Year by *Sports Illustrated*.

Michael Jordan is one of only three players to have either more 2,000-point seasons or to lead the league in field goals made more often than James.

CAREER RANKINGS
[REGULAR SEASON AND POST-SEASON RANKINGS]

James ranks high on different lists for all-time and current NBA players in several categories, including:

MOST SEASONS WITH 2,000 OR MORE POINTS SCORED (REGULAR SEASON)

Player Name	Number of Seasons
Karl Malone	12
Michael Jordan	11
LeBron James	**10**

MOST SEASONS LEADING THE LEAGUE IN FIELD GOALS MADE (REGULAR SEASON)

Player Name	Number of Seasons
Michael Jordan	10
Wilt Chamberlain	7
LeBron James	5
Shaquille O'Neal	5
Kareem Abdul-Jabbar	5

James has a long way to go to catch free throws–made record holder Karl "The Mailman" Malone.

FREE THROWS MADE (REGULAR SEASON CAREER)

Player Name	Free Throws Made
Karl Malone*	9,787
Moses Malone*	9,018
Kobe Bryant	8,378
LeBron James (Ranked Eigth All-Time)	**7,140**

Based on his season average of 457 free throws made, it would take James another 524 games (about six-and-one-third seasons) to pass current career record holder Karl Malone. He is currently the active career free throws–made leader.

FIELD GOALS MADE (REGULAR SEASON CAREER)

Player Name	Field Goals Made
Kareem Abdul-Jabbar*	15,837
Karl Malone*	13,528
Wilt Chamberlain*	12,681
LeBron James (Ranked Fifth All-Time)	**11,838**

Based on his season average of 752 field goals made, it would take James another 497 games (about six seasons) to pass current career record holder Kareem Abdul-Jabbar.

ASSISTS MADE (REGULAR SEASON CAREER)

Player Name	Assists Made
John Stockton*	15,806
Jason Kidd*	12,091
Steve Nash*	10,335
Mark Jackson	10,334
LeBron James (Ranked tenth All-Time)	**8,662**

*indicates member of the NBA Hall of Fame.

Based on his season average of 547 assists, it would take James another 1,138-½ games (about 14 seasons) to pass current career record holder John Stockton. He is currently the second active career assist leader (behind Chris Paul of the Houston Rockets).

James also ranks fourth all-time in number of playoff games played (239), 20 behind career leader Derek Fisher who is at 259. He is the all-time leader in career playoff minutes played (10,049), which is 679 minutes (fourteen games) more than the next player, Tim Duncan (formerly of the San Antonio Spurs). He is the career playoff leader in field goals made with 2,457 (101 more field goals than the next player, Kareem Abdul-Jabbar), and 1,627 free throws made (164 more than Michael Jordan), and is third all-time in career playoff assists with 1,687 (behind Hall of Famers Magic Johnson and John Stockton with 2,346 and 1,839, respectively).

James is tenth all-time in career assists, but he is barely halfway to the total of NBA career assist record holder John Stockton.

LeBron James stands for the national anthem.

BRINGING HOME THE GOLD

The US Men's National Basketball Team turned in a disappointing bronze-medal performance at the 2004 Summer Olympics games in Athens, Greece. The team, which featured James, the youngest member at age nineteen, lost three games for the first time in Olympic history. After an opening loss to Puerto Rico, and losses to Lithuania and Argentina, the U.S. settled for a third-place finish in a rematch victory over the Lithuanian national team. James for his part scored a total of 43 points in eight games for an average of 5.4 points per game along with eight rebounds and 13 assists.

The 2008 Olympics in Beijing, China, gave James an opportunity for redemption. James took the team, nicknamed the "Redeem Team" by the media, on his back, averaging 15.5 points in each of the eight games he played. His effort helped the U.S. reclaim its position as the best in the world as the team went on to beat Spain for the gold. He came back one more time in the 2012 London games where he averaged 13.2 points and again helped lead the U.S. to a gold-medal victory over Spain.

It appears to be a question of not if LeBron James will go down as the greatest basketball player (both in the NBA and in the world) but, when he retires, by how much he will be ahead of all others who have played the game.

The only blemish on his career is a 3-6 record in the NBA Finals. Michael Jordan, for example, was 6-0 on the sport's biggest stage. At age thirty-four (at the end of the 2018–2019 NBA season) James still has time to add to his incredible on-court résumé.

 # TEXT-DEPENDENT QUESTIONS

1. How many times was James named to the NBA All-Defensive first team?

2. Where does he rank among active players on the career free throws–made list?

3. What year(s) did he win an Olympic gold medal as a member of the US Men's National Basketball team? How many Olympic medals (total) has he won?

 # RESEARCH PROJECT

James has accomplished a lot on the court in his career. He is one of only a handful of players to excel at the game coming straight from high school. How does his career compare to some of the other players that have chosen to come to the NBA directly from high school? Look at the career of other current (or former) high school players drafted in the first round, compare their offensive (i.e., field goals, two-point shots made, three-point shots made, assists, rebounds) statistics, and compile a top five list of players who graduated directly to the NBA.

WORDS TO UNDERSTAND

denounce: To declare (especially publicly) as blameworthy or evil

dependency: The state of being reliant on someone or something else for aid, support, etc.

offspring: Children or young of a particular parent

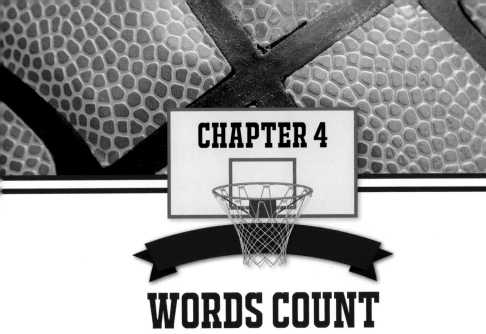

CHAPTER 4

WORDS COUNT

When the time comes to address the media before or after a game, players either retreat to the comfort of traditional phrases that avoid controversy (Cliché City), or they speak their mind with refreshing candor (Quote Machine).

Here are 10 quotes, compiled in part from the website Brainyquote. com, with some insight as to the context of what James is talking about or referencing:

"You can't be afraid to fail. It's the only way you succeed—you're not gonna succeed all the time, and I know that."

James has been successful throughout his time in the NBA, having earned four MVP awards and won three NBA championships (two as a member of the Miami Heat and one with the Cleveland Cavaliers). He understands that success comes with knowing that there always exists a possibility for failure. As many times as he has won the championship (in 2012, 2013, and 2016), he has also failed to achieve his goal on six other occasions (in 2007, 2011, 2014, 2015, 2017, and 2018). James also failed to lend much insight into his ups and downs with this tried and true cliché. **Rating: Cliché City**

In his four seasons with Miami, James won two championships, and also lost twice in the finals.

"My mom and I have always been there for each other. We had some tough times, but she was always there for me."

James grew up the only offspring of Anthony McClelland and Gloria Marie James, and after his father left the family, it was only Gloria and LeBron left to take care of each other. The two have an incredibly close bond that has been developed through years of dependency on one another to survive the harsh economic times they faced growing up in Akron, Ohio. James is very loyal to his mother and appreciative of her being there to help shape him into the man that he has become. It is not a unique story in the league, and James certainly did not lend anything unique to its telling with this quote. **Rating: Cliché City**

> **"I don't know how tall I am or how much I weigh. Because I don't want anybody to know my identity. I'm like a superhero. Call me Basketball Man."**

James jokes here that as a "superhero" of sorts, he likes to keep his identity secret. What he means with this quote is that he likes to keep it a secret as to what he plans to do when on the court. He can take on the role of scoring, blocking shots, stealing the ball, and dishing the ball to other players on the team to get them involved in the game, and display the leadership skills and passion for winning that have made him successful. **Rating: Quote Machine**

> **"You know, God gave me a gift to do other things besides play the game of basketball."**

He has benefited from his talent on the basketball court but understands that his gifts, and the responsibilities that come with the visibility they bring, go beyond the game. James operates a charitable foundation that provides opportunities for underserved youth and has placed a focus and emphasis on creating educational opportunities for urban youth (see more in Chapter 5). He fully understands that it is his responsibility to use his fame and celebrity to give back to the community he left to become a great NBA player. **Rating: Quote Machine**

Despite all his success on the basketball court, James is dedicated to giving back to the community that allowed him to achieve his dreams.

"I have short goals—to get better every day, to help my teammates every day—but my only ultimate goal is to win an NBA championship. It's all that matters. I dream about it. I dream about it all the time, how it would look, how it would feel. It would be so amazing."

The desire James had to win was evident early in his career, but he did eventually realize his ultimate goal in 2012. James has a three-win, six-loss record in NBA Finals, having also won in 2013 and 2016. Winning the NBA championship has been the height of his career, but losing six times has stuck with him like a thorn in what has otherwise been a great career, to this point. He has often been compared to Michael Jordan and is arguably one of, if not the, greatest players in NBA history. Jordan won six NBA championships in his 21 seasons with the Chicago Bulls and Washington Wizards. James will need to add several more NBA championship trophies to his collection if he hopes to rival the six collected by Jordan. **Rating: Quote Machine**

"My father wasn't around when I was a kid, and I used to always say, 'Why me? Why don't I have a father? Why isn't he around? Why did he leave my mother?' But as I got older I looked deeper and thought, 'I don't know what my father was going through, but if he was around all the time, would I be who I am today?'"

James grew up with his mother Gloria and did not have the presence of a father to guide him as he grew older and became an adult. He reflects in this quote about how it felt growing up without a father. He is expressing thoughts of sadness and regret as to why his father did not want to be with him and his mother but also recognizes that he may or may not be the person (and player) that he has become if his father had stayed with the family. **Rating: Quote Machine**

"Basketball is my passion, I love it. But my family and friends mean everything to me. That's what's important."

James discusses the priority he places on having good friends and the love of his family above playing basketball. He maintains constant contact with his loved ones and stays reminded of how important they are to him and also to remind him why he plays the game in the first place. Family first is a nice, if unoriginal, sentiment. **Rating: Cliché City**

"You know, my family and friends have never been yes-men: 'Yes, you're doing the right thing, you're always right.' No, they tell me when I'm wrong, and that's why I've been able to stay who I am and stay humble."

James, seen here with his wife Savannah Brinson at a 2015 movie premier, puts his family above all else.

James is regarded as a superstar in the sport of basketball. Given how big a star he is, it would be easy for him to simply surround himself with people that only agree with him and do not challenge him in any way. He is appreciative of the fact that the type of people in his life are not just those who constantly praise him and his talent. He surrounds himself with people, friends, and family who are willing to call him out when he is wrong or challenge the way he looks at things to help him be a better person. **Rating: Quote Machine**

James has scored more than 30,000 career points, but his 8,000-plus career assists show that he is an unselfish player.

"I've always been an unselfish guy, and that's the only way I know how to play on the court, and I try to play to the maximum of my ability—not only for myself but for my teammates."

James has an overwhelming desire to win. Although he is ranked number four for most points scored in an NBA career (32,543), he is also the only player with more than 30,000 points scored, 8,000 total rebounds, and 8,000 assists. These numbers show that he is willing to not only take over a game and score points but that he is also willing to dish the ball to other players and get them involved in the game. This unselfish nature allowed him to play well alongside fellow 2003 NBA draft picks Chris Bosh and Dwyane Wade, both pretty good scorers themselves, and win consecutive championships in 2012 and 2013 for the Miami Heat. **Rating: Quote Machine**

> **"My game is really played above time. I don't say that like I'm saying I'm ahead of my time. I'm saying, like, if I'm on the court and I throw a pass, the ball that I've thrown will lead my teammate right where he needs to go, before he even knows that that's the right place to go to."**

This quote is similar to one by hockey great Wayne Gretzky who said, "I don't skate to where the puck is at but to where the puck is going to be." This means that James (like Gretzky) plays the game with an eye toward the next shot, next play, or next defensive setup. This way of looking at the game is a show of his leadership skills and is why he is often considered a coach on the court, helping his teammates be in the best situation to defend or score.
Rating: Quote Machine

THE DECISION

James decided to test the free agency waters when his contract with the Cleveland Cavaliers came up at the end of the 2009–2010 season. After he considered staying with his hometown Cavaliers to continue his career, he decided to accept an offer to join the Miami Heat.

The decision to leave Ohio and the Cavaliers was a difficult one for him to make. The way this decision was handled, however, sparked controversy. James scheduled a televised live event (titled, *The Decision*) on July 8, 2010, on the ESPN network to announce his free-agency decision to leave Cleveland for Miami. The televised special ran for 75 minutes, featuring highlights of his career to that point and his efforts to bring a championship to Cleveland. James was heavily criticized for what was widely regarded as a publicity stunt. He knew he was going to Miami before free agency began but left all interested teams, including his own, in limbo for a week. James was vilified in Cleveland, and his popularity plummeted as a result of *The Decision*.

The way James announced he was joining the Heat in free agency for the 2010-2011 season was unpopular and highly criticized.

His decision to leave Ohio was fueled by a desire to not only win in the regular season but also to win championships. As James said during the broadcast, "I'm going to take my talents to South Beach and join the Miami Heat. I feel like it's going to give me the best opportunity to win and to win for multiple years, and not only just to win in the regular season or just to win five games in a row or three games in a row. I want to be able to win championships. And I feel like I can compete down there."

THE FAMOUS "DECISION"

James became a free agent at the end of the 2010 NBA season, which allowed him to negotiate with other teams interested in having him play for them. Although he had played his seven seasons with the Cleveland Cavaliers and was believed to be re-signing with the team, he surprised everyone with a televised event aired on ESPN called *The Decision*. It was during this program that James announced that he was joining players Dwyane Wade and Chris Bosh as members of the Miami Heat. The decision met with a lot of criticism from fans and former players such as legends Michael Jordan and Magic Johnson. It also prompted an open letter to Cleveland fans from Cavaliers owner Dan Gilbert, who **denounced** James publicly. James, years later, expressed regret for the way he handled the announcement.

James, appearing in his televised special with sportscaster Jim Gray on July 8, 2010, announcing his decision to sign with the Miami Heat. The program raised a total of $6 million for charity, including $2.5 million that went to the Greenwich, Connecticut, Boys & Girls Club, where the broadcast took place.

TEXT-DEPENDENT QUESTIONS

1. How many NBA championships did LeBron James win through the 2017–2018 season? Has he won more or less championships than former Chicago Bull and Washington Wizard Michael Jordan?

2. What NBA team did James choose to join in 2010?

3. Which two NBA stars did James team up with in 2010?

 # RESEARCH PROJECT

James won NBA championships while a member of two different NBA franchises, the Cleveland Cavaliers (who initially drafted him in 2003) and the Miami Heat. He joins a group of players who have won championships with more than one team. Make a list of at least 10 players who have won multiple championships with two or more NBA teams. List the player, the teams they played for, and the year(s) they won the championship with that team. As a hint, James is chasing one of those players for the all-time career scoring lead and is coached by the son of another.

 WORDS TO UNDERSTAND

affluent: Having an abundance of wealth, property, or other material goods; prosperous; rich

persona: A person's perceived or evident personality, such as that of a well-known official, actor, or celebrity; personal image; public role

thespian: An actor or actress

CHAPTER 5

OFF THE COURT

LIFE AT HOME

LeBron James married his long-time girlfriend and high school sweetheart, Savannah Brinson, in a ceremony held in San Diego, California, on September 14, 2013. The couple have three children together, two sons LeBron, Jr. (born in 2004) and Bryce Maximus (born in 2007), and a daughter, Zhuri Nova, who was born in 2014.

James has felt it an important part of his persona to be a strong fatherly role model for his children, particularly to his sons, as he did not grow up with such a role model when he was a youth. The couple and their children live in a spacious, 9,300-plus-square-foot home in the affluent Los Angeles neighborhood of Brentwood. Having purchased the home in 2015 (for a reported price of $21 million) it fits well with his decision to join the Los Angeles Lakers.

James married his high school sweetheart, Savannah Brinson, in 2013.

LEBRON JAMES FAMILY FOUNDATION

James, after his first year as a member of the Cleveland Cavaliers, formed the LeBron James Family Foundation. Based in Cleveland, the mission of the foundation "is to positively affect the lives of children and young adults through education and co-curricular educational initiatives. We believe that an education and living an active, healthy lifestyle is pivotal to the development of children and young adults."

The foundation has created important partnerships with organizations such as the Boys & Girls Club, his high school alma mater St. Vincent–St. Mary High School, and Akron Public Schools, among others, to provide opportunities essential for leveling the playing field for all children, regardless of income. He has renovated his high school gym, provided scholarships, and, through his all-star weekend ambassador program, has engaged in community service projects in and around the greater Akron area.

His foundation is supportive of efforts to bring STEM (Science, Technology, Engineering, and Math) education to low-income students, focusing on the use of technology and increasing computer access. He also advocates expanding opportunities for students to learn math and computer programming, essential skills for competing in an ever-changing global environment.

THE IMPORTANCE OF EDUCATION

LeBron James entered the NBA in 2003 after attending St. Vincent–St. Mary High School in Akron, Ohio. He received offers from several schools to play basketball but never attended college. Although he did not go to college, James strongly believes in the importance of education. This is demonstrated by his commitment to invest more than $41 million from his private foundation

THE
I PROMISE
SCHOOL

to fund a school effort called "I Promise" that is geared toward providing greater opportunities for those at risk.

James has also created important partnerships with organizations such as the Boys & Girls Club (an important organization to him while he was growing up), his alma mater St. Vincent–St. Mary High School, the Akron Public Schools, and various other community-based groups. James makes himself available to speak with students and has put his money where his mouth is in terms of his commitment to improve the community where he grew up. The foundation's all-star weekend in Akron provides an opportunity for his "ambassadors" to engage in community service projects designed to improve lives and further his personal mission to help make a difference in people's lives.

FULFILLING THE DREAM FOR OTHERS, "I PROMISE"

One example of the support James gives to education is his creation of the I Promise School in Akron. James announced the opening of the school in August 2018. The school plans to do more for its students than most public school do in that it will provide free uniforms and transportation, as well as free bicycles and helmets to students, food (breakfast, lunch, and snacks) to ensure full attention in class, and free tuition for graduates to attend the University of Akron.

The model for the school is based on his own childhood experience. He was given the opportunity to excel in school because of the support he received from coaches and other adults in his life who encouraged him to become the best person, not just the best basketball player, that he could be. The I Promise School looks to provide students with what James refers to as the three-pointer in opportunity for education, "financial capital to buffer against poverty, human capital like skills and credentials to compete in today's economy, and social capital, or supportive relationships, to help young people get by and get ahead."

Watch this discussion between ESPN reporter Rachel Nichols and anchor Scott Van Pelt about the I Promise School in Akron, Ohio.

LeBron James opens public school in Akron for at-risk children

MARKETING LEBRON JAMES

James is represented by the Fenway Sports Group, LLC, located in Boston, Massachusetts. The company was founded in 2001 by Tom Werner and John W. Henry. Many know Tom Werner as half of the Hollywood production team Carsey-Werner that produced some of the most successful television comedies ever made. He and Henry are co-owners of the Boston Red Sox baseball team, and Fenway Sports Group is the parent company of the Red Sox.

James struck a deal with Fenway Sports Group in April of 2011 to make the group his exclusive marketing representative. This partnership, along with his LRMR Branding & Marketing company, gave him part ownership in the group's soccer franchise, Liverpool (England) Football Club of the English Premier League. It also helps James expand his image globally and make the most of his successes on the court as well as provide additional income to fund many of the initiatives and community projects that he is involved in away from the court.

He signed a four-year deal with the Los Angeles Lakers in 2018 for more than $154 million, making him one of the highest-paid athletes in the world. He also receives $42 million annually in endorsement deals with many different companies and their products. These deals include:

- Audemars Piguet

- Coca-Cola

- Dunkin' Donuts

Tom Werner (L) is minority owner of the Boston Red Sox baseball team and the agency that represents James.

James wears Nike apparel during a 2012 visit to Arlington National Cemetery in Virginia. Nike is one of his primary sponsors.

- Nike

- Samsung

- Upper Deck

LEBRON JAMES THE PERFORMER

James has had many opportunities to expand his horizons off the court. In addition to the countless interviews and specials that he has been featured in that have honored his efforts on the basketball court, he has had opportunities to produce several shows. He is the executive producer and star of the remake of the Warner Brothers film, *Space Jam*. The original *Space Jam*, a live-animated action film, featured Michael Jordan and Bugs Bunny. James takes on Michael Jordan's role in the new version.

James also played himself in the 2015 movie *Trainwreck* starring Amy Schumer and Bill Hader. He demonstrated his skills as a **thespian** playing the part of best friend and advice-giver to Hader's character and held his own against the talents of Hader, a former member of the cast of *Saturday Night Live*, and Schumer, famously known for her comedy specials and self-titled show.

James poses with the character Migo at the 2018 premier of *Smallfoot*, a movie in which James was a lead voice performer.

TEXT-DEPENDENT QUESTIONS

1. Where did LeBron James decide to locate his school for at-risk students?

2. What is the name of the project his foundation provided $41 million in funding to improve opportunities for low-income students in Akron, Ohio?

3. In which English Premier League team does he have an ownership interest?

RESEARCH PROJECT

James, through his marketing partnership with Fenway Sports Group, LLC, is a part-owner of the Liverpool Football Club. He is one of a number of NBA players (past and present) who have ownership interest in a professional sports franchise. Find at least four other NBA players and the name of the franchise they own. Hint: The player may be in the league currently or a retired player. The sports franchise can be in the U.S. or in another country.

assist: a pass that directly leads to a teammate making a basket.

blocked shot: when a defensive player stops a shot at the basket by hitting the ball away.

center: a player whose main job is to score near the basket and win offensive and defensive rebounds. Centers are usually the tallest players on the court, and the best are able to move with speed and agility.

double dribble: when a player dribbles the ball with two hands or stops dribbling and starts again. The opposing team gets the ball.

field goal: a successful shot worth 2 points—3 points if shot from behind the three-point line.

foul: called by the officials for breaking a rule: reaching in, blocking, charging, and over the back, for example. If a player commits six fouls during the game, he fouls out and must leave play. If an offensive player is fouled while shooting, he usually gets two foul shots (one shot if the player's basket counted or three if he was fouled beyond the three-point line).

foul shot: a "free throw," an uncontested shot taken from the foul line (15 feet [4.6 m]) from the basket.

goaltending: when a defensive player touches the ball after it has reached its highest point on the way to the basket. The team on offense gets the points they would have received from the basket. Goaltending is also called on any player, on offense or defense, who slaps the backboard or touches the ball directly above the basket.

jump ball: when an official puts the ball into play by tossing it in the air. Two opposing players try to tip it to their own teammate.

man-to-man defense: when each defensive player guards a single offensive player.

officials: those who monitor the action and call fouls. In the NBA there are three for each game.

point guard: the player who handles the ball most on offense. He brings the ball up the court and tries to create scoring opportunities through passing. Good point guards are quick, good passers, and can see the court well.

power forward: a player whose main jobs are to score from close to the basket and win offensive and defensive rebounds. Good power forwards are tall and strong.

rebound: when a player gains possession of the ball after a missed shot.

roster: the players on a team. NBA teams have 12-player rosters.

shooting guard: a player whose main job is to score using jump shots and drives to the basket. Good shooting guards are usually taller than point guards but still quick.

shot clock: a 24-second clock that starts counting down when a team gets the ball. The clock restarts whenever the ball changes possession. If the offense does not shoot the ball in time, it turns the ball over to the other team.

small forward: a player whose main job is to score from inside or outside. Good small forwards are taller than point or shooting guards and have speed and agility.

steal: when a defender takes the ball from an opposing player.

technical foul: called by the official for misconduct or a procedural violation. The team that does not commit the foul gets possession of the ball and a free throw.

three-point play: a two-point field goal combined with a successful free throw. This happens when an offensive player makes a basket but is fouled in the process.

three-point shot: a field goal made from behind the three-point line.

traveling: when a player moves, taking three steps or more, without dribbling, also called "walking." The opposing team gets the ball.

turnover: when the offensive team loses the ball: passing the ball out of bounds, traveling, or double dribbling, for example.

zone defense: when each defensive player guards within a specific area of the court. Common zones include 2-1-2, 1-3-1, or 2-3. Zone defense has only recently been allowed in the NBA.

FURTHER READING

Brendan, Bowers, and Jones, Ryan. *LeBron James vs. the NBA: The Case for the NBA's Greatest Player*. Chicago: Triumph Books, 2017.

Ciovacco, Justine. *LeBron James: NBA Champion*. Chicago: Encyclopaedia Britannica, 2015.

Lloyd, Jason. *The Blueprint: LeBron James, Cleveland's Deliverance, and the Making of the Modern NBA*. Westminster, UK: Penguin, 2017.

Savage, Jeff. *LeBron James, 4th Edition*. Minneapolis, MN: Lerner Publications, 2016.

Windhorst, Brian, and McMenamin, Dave. *Return of the King: LeBron James, the Cleveland Cavaliers and the Greatest Comeback in NBA History*. New York City: Grand Central Publishing, 2017.

INTERNET RESOURCES

https://www.basketball-reference.com/players/j/jamesle01.html
The basketball-specific resource provided by Sports Reference LLC for LeBron James' current and historical statistics.

http://bleacherreport.com/nba
The official website for Bleacher Report Sport's NBA reports on each of the 30 teams.

https://www.cbssports.com/nba/teams/page/LAL/los-angeles-lakers
The web page for the Los Angeles Lakers provided by CBSSports.com, providing latest news and information, player profiles, scheduling, and standings.

http://www.latimes.com/sports/lakers/
The *Los Angeles Times* newspaper's web page for the Los Angeles Lakers basketball team.

http://www.espn.com/nba/team/_/name/lal/los-angeles-lakers
The official website of ESPN sports network for the Los Angeles Lakers.

http://www.nba.com/#/
The official website of the National Basketball Association.

https://www.nba.com/lakers/
The official website for the Los Angeles Lakers basketball team, including history, player information, statistics, and news.

https://sports.yahoo.com/nba/
The official website of Yahoo! Sports NBA coverage, providing news, statistics, and important information about the association and its 30 teams.

INDEX

INDEX

INDEX

EDUCATIONAL VIDEO LINKS

Pg. 12: http://x-qr.net/1G0G

Pg. 13: http://x-qr.net/1D3z

Pg. 14: http://x-qr.net/1DJt

Pg. 15: http://x-qr.net/1Hew

Pg. 16: http://x-qr.net/1GAp

Pg. 17: http://x-qr.net/1E8J

Pg. 18: http://x-qr.net/1D3E

Pg. 19: http://x-qr.net/1DZp

Pg. 30: http://x-qr.net/1G2P

Pg. 45: http://x-qr.net/1DWh

Pg. 62: http://x-qr.net/1GdR

Pg. 69: http://x-qr.net/1EMb

PHOTO CREDITS

AUTHOR BIOGRAPHY

Donald Parker is an avid sports fan, author, and father. He enjoys watching and participating in many types of sports, including football, basketball, baseball, and golf. He enjoyed a brief career as a punter and defensive back at NCAA Division III Carroll College (now University) in Waukesha, Wisconsin, and spends much of his time now watching and writing about the sports he loves.